I0518717

BODYCAM

ALEXANDER ENGEL-HODGKINSON

ALEXANDER ENGEL-HODGKINSON

BODYCAM
Copyright © 2021 by Alexander Engel-Hodgkinson
All rights reserved.
1st paperback edition
ISBN 978-1-989331-19-4
Cover art by Alexander Engel-Hodgkinson

Published by
Dark Brothers Incorporated

PARENTAL ADVISORY

This book contains graphic violence and profanity, and disturbing sexual themes intended for mature readers aged 17 and up.

AUTHOR'S COMMENT

A short story idea had been rattling around in my brain that was part *Videodrome*, part *8MM*. Somehow I got this.

ALEXANDER ENGEL-HODGKINSON

BODYCAM

BODYCAM

SUNDAY/MARCH 9ᵀᴴ/1997
AM 00:03:00:44

I woke up with a scream, searching the darkness of my room in fearful confusion. A nightmare? If so, I couldn't remember what the hell it was about. I felt like I always did after having a nightmare— that uneasy feeling, the paranoia that hadn't passed yet. Like something was there, in the room, waiting for me to spot its outline lurking in plain sight in the shadows of my room. I glanced around in search for it, but there was nothing there. I reached over to feel her shoulder, but my hand fell on an empty expanse of sheets. Right. A pang of grief struck me as I suddenly remembered why the other half of the bed was unoccupied.

Elaine…

I turned over and cried myself back to sleep. I had a dream about Elaine, about how she used to dance like a ballerina on the patio stones for a good laugh. She was good at it; too good for it to be just a joke, but that's all it was to her. I prodded her good-naturedly sometimes, telling her she should go pro, maybe open up a dance academy in Freiburg, Germany. She didn't appreciate the obscure reference, but that was okay. In my dream, her hair flowed in the wind like waves of silk. It was longer than she ever kept it in real life. She was beautiful; the kind of woman any guy would think was out of his league. I knew I was lucky that she loved me, too. I wasn't particularly good-looking, and I wasn't a very interesting man, either. She danced and I was mesmerized by her slow gyrations, her calculated spins. Everything else seemed to melt away around us, revealing someone standing rigidly from afar, watching us. I squinted, trying to look past Elaine, but I couldn't make out any physical details of the figure. It was too far away. Elaine stopped dancing and asked me if I'd had enough of her performance, but, just for the moment, I wasn't listening. She asked what I was looking at, and when she turned, the figure ducked seemingly into thin air.

At six, I awoke to the sound of hissing and turned over to see static snow on the TV. I didn't recall turning it on. I stared at it and watched the shadows dance

<u>BODYCAM</u>

in the hailstorm. White noise filled my ears as the shadows linked to form a face distended in agony. I blinked a few times and peered closer.

Just snow. And white noise.

I turned the TV off, set the percolator so that I had some coffee brewing while I hopped into the shower and dressed. I read the first three stories in *Shock II,* by Richard Matheson. When I was on my third cup, I glanced at the clock on the wall on the wall above the kitchen sink and saw that it was almost seven.

I got up and went into Heather's bedroom and gently shook her awake. She was six years old—turning seven in June. I had her get dressed while I made oatmeal. We sat down at the table and ate in silence. She paused every few minutes to rub sleep from her eyes or yawn.

Short bangs of hazelnut hair framed her pretty little face and big, bright green eyes. She looked just like her mom. She was a little angel, rarely misbehaved, usually just made mistakes, like all kids do. Can't fault kids for making mistakes.

"How was your sleep?" I asked her.

"Fine." She scooped more cereal into her mouth. Milk spilled down her chin.

"That's good. Honey, you're making a mess."

She dabbed her face with a napkin and smiled at me. "All better."

"Good girl." I sipped my coffee. "Any bad dreams?"

"No."

"No bad dreams. Good. Did Marley keep the bad dreams away?"

She nodded, beaming.

"He's a good bear. Good Marley."

"Good Marley!"

We went to the funeral service at St. Michael's Baptist Church about a ten-minute drive away. I was never any kind of believer, but Elaine was. We never missed a Sunday service until three weeks ago, when Elaine was attacked, and…

Heather didn't seem to notice that we'd stopped going, or didn't seem to care. Maybe she was lost in her own thoughts, wondering what could have happened, when her mother would be home from the hospital. It bothered her a little—she'd ask

8

BODYCAM

me where mommy was every day—but she never even considered the possibility that mommy would never come home until I told her a week after the plug was pulled.

I couldn't keep up that charade for long. She kept asking if we could visit her in the hospital. I had enough excuses to fill a book ready to go, but somehow she seemed to always ask me at the wrong times. I was never prepared for it, even when I thought I was.

So I told her. I told her she wasn't coming back. She went to heaven.

Every long, empty day since then, every time I looked into her little eyes, I saw fresh tears.

Turning off the engine of my Audi 5000 four-door in the parking lot, I watched worshippers of Christ milling about the church's front steps in their Sunday best. Friends in the community. My family didn't like Elaine, and they couldn't be bothered to drive six hundred kilometres. Elaine was an orphan and an only child, so she had no family to mourn her passing.

So it was the community that came to offer their condolences and their respects.

ALEXANDER ENGEL-HODGKINSON

The Crawfords and their two kids. The Cavanaughs and their teenage daughter. The elderly Boyds. The Silverburghs and their three little boys. Ms. Maria and her daughter. The Morgans with their two young sons and one-year-old daughter. The Petersons, the wife expecting their first in a couple weeks. The Wilsons and the Williamsons and their two children each. Naturally, my least favourites were there as well: the Andersons with their twenty-something son and five-year-old daughter.

Heather, sitting impatiently in the back seat, asked if we were going in. I sighed, hesitant, and told her yes. We got out and held hands all the way to the front door as mourners started filing inside, each greeted personally by Pastor Lawrence Clemens and his wife, Andrea. We waited awkwardly as the Cavanaugh girl spoke eagerly to Clemens about improvements in her math exam, all thanks to Andrea's tutelage. She was a bubbly little thing, her excitement and happiness nearly infectious. Clemens beamed proudly at that, as Mrs. Cavanaugh crowded him and thanked him alongside her daughter. I considered

BODYCAM

walking around them, but the entrance was too jammed up. Luckily, we didn't have to wait long before the Cavanaughs went inside. I shook Clemens' hand. He said it was good to see me and asked if I was doing okay, being discreet around the little one. I knew what he meant. I said I was fine. He greeted Heather and asked her how she was doing. She stepped behind me shyly and said that she was good.

Clemens had handled the funeral arrangements for me, with my input, to ease my mind. I appreciated that. We were closer to Clemens and his family than anyone else in the community. To them, losing Elaine was like losing a sibling.

In the coatroom, I noticed the Anderson boy stooped down, speaking to Heather in hushed tones. Even in a Sunday suit, he looked grungy and oily, with strange, squinty eyes, dishevelled black hair, and skin that shone with an oily sheen under the ceiling lights, like he was breaking into sweats. He said something, smiling, and it looked to me like he was leering over her. He pinched her cheek, still smiling. I was about to call her when

ALEXANDER ENGEL-HODGKINSON

Mrs. Donna Anderson's blonde bowl cut dipped into my field of vision, her big blue-eyed smile disgustingly artificial and condescending. She blocked my view of her boy and my daughter, asking me questions like how I was doing (I said I'll live), how I was doing (I said I've been better), how Heather was taking it (I said she was doing okay), how much did she know about... well, you know (I said enough), and then she asked me when I'd get married again because there's plenty of fish in the sea (I told her to get out of my way).

"Excuse me?" She seemed taken aback.

"Get out of my way, please. I'm going inside with my daughter." I sidled past her.

"Now, hold on." She reached out and grabbed my shoulder.

I turned right around. I glared at her. I told her, very quietly so as not to disturb the peace in the lobby: "Fuck off."

She backed down and called her son over. I took Heather's hand and led her into the sanctuary and we sat as far away

BODYCAM

from the Anderson's as was humanly possible. I hated those creeps. With Elaine gone, there was no possible means of maintaining a distant, sociable relationship with them. I don't know how she could stand those snobs. Even now, glancing across the sanctuary, I could see Donna whispering heatedly to her stoic husband about how I'd ruined her morning. Yes. How dare I talk to her with such disrespect? I couldn't tell if he was ignoring her or just keeping up appearances by staring forward at the altar while Clemens delivered his sermon.

Her son was sitting on the other side of her, leaning forward just far enough so that he could stare back at me past his parents. Little creep. He was the reason I kept Heather close to me during service, instead of allowing her to go to Sunday school with the other children. She scribbled into a colouring book on the pew next to me.

After the service, after everyone in the church and their cousin, it seemed, had offered their sympathies; Pastor Clemens approached me again. It was like he actively searched for me in the crowd, and when he found me and Heather in the coatroom he offered his extended condolences once more. Unlike the Andersons, I liked Clemens, and I'd welcomed him and his wife as warmly as Elaine had. We all got along. He seemed earnest in everything he said.

"If there's anything you need," he told me, "if you need a friend to talk to, or something, just give me a call. I'll be more than happy to invite you and Heather over for dinner. Or, if you prefer, I'll pay a social visit sometime. Even a phone call would be okay—the *occasional* phone call, not a thousand every month." He chuckled dryly. "Andrea and I would love to have you."

"Thank you, Lawrence. I appreciate it. Really. But I'm just... just not in a good headspace right now."

He smiled warmly and patted my shoulder. "Hey. I understand. When you're able, when you're in the mood for company, give me a call." He slipped me his card with his office phone number on it, which I pocketed.

14

BODYCAM

In the car during the drive home, I asked Heather what that Anderson boy said to her. She didn't answer me right away. I said her name, prodding her. She said he wanted to play later.

"Listen, kiddo… I want you to tell me exactly what he said to you."

She hesitated.

"You're not in trouble," I assured her. "I just want to know what he said."

Visibly relieved, she gave me an answer: "He said he was trying to convince his mom to invite us over for dinner so that he could show me his cool toys, and his computer lab, and his QuickCam. He wanted to show me all of his stuff in his lab. Can we go, Daddy?"

That made me so uncomfortable. I felt my discomfort curdle in the pit of my stomach. "No."

She started to pout. "Pleeease?"

"I said no."

We stopped going to church after that.

SUNDAY/APRIL 6TH/1997
AM 00:03:33:55

I woke in a cold sweat. I couldn't tell you why I did; I just did. I looked at the clock and balked at the time. Christ. Three in the morning, and I was already wide awake. Did I have a nightmare? If so, I couldn't remember it, and I couldn't be sure of the reason for my abrupt awakening. I tried to remember what it was, but I couldn't come up with anything.

I saw eyes wide with fear staring across my bedroom at me. I blinked, feeling my heart freeze in my chest, but it melted when I realized it was just my wife's beautiful smile frozen in time in our wedding photo. I got up and pressed the photo face down on the dresser and went back to bed.

I couldn't escape the feeling that I was being watched by something that was moving around in here; the air felt different. I couldn't explain it. But there was *something* and it was *here*. I glanced over at the window by the TV set. I got up and checked the window. Locked. I turned on

BODYCAM

every light in the house as I searched every room with a bat, checked every window, every door. All locked.

It's been two months and I still hadn't gotten used to sleeping alone. I knew I had to adjust if I valued my sanity. That was all that mattered now.

Sometimes it still felt like she was here. Her presence seemed to linger in the small hours. But it wasn't the same. Not since I found what was left of her in front of the TV. She was waiting for me to come home from work when she fell asleep watching tapes.

That's when he struck. Someone broke in and took her from me. He violated her and tormented her. She was never the same. She didn't speak. She didn't blink. She's been in the hospital ever since. "Certified braindead," they later told me. He took her life that day, and didn't have the decency to kill her. No. He left her that way, in that state, like that was how he wanted her. Like knowing what he'd done was what turned him on. She wasn't the first in the area, the police said, and she wouldn't be the last. They were sure of that.

Heather and I hadn't been sleeping much lately. Heather's too young to understand what her mother went through, and I couldn't bring myself to explain why her mom couldn't come home. Not truthfully, anyway. I said she was unwell, which I guess was kind of true. A gross understatement, but it was all I could say without breaking down in front of her.

I found Elaine lying naked in a pool of blood and filth, her eyes wide and unfocused, staring at the static snow on the TV screen.

I sat where I'd found her at the foot of the queen-size bed and now I was the one who stared into the static snow on the TV screen. I peered deep into the white noise image, seeing shapes dancing provocatively in the blizzard like distorted ballerinas. They twisted and twirled and groped themselves and made obscene movements with their hands over their private parts.

I couldn't remember when I turned the TV on. I stood up and turned it off, plunging me into total darkness. That's when I realized the lights were off. Perhaps

BODYCAM

I'd switched them off after my search and just forgot about it, or something. I was tired, after all. It was nearly four in the morning now.

I went to check on Heather. She was sound asleep in her bed hugging Marley close to her. Something moved in her window and I looked out into the backyard as a shape darted around to the side of the house. I went into my room and grabbed the .38 snubnose revolver from the top drawer of my dresser as I heard the unmistakable rapid-fire report of feet pounding across the front porch. I peered through the window above the bed but no one was there. The mailbox at the end of the driveway clanked shut. I knew it was the mailbox because it had a very distinctive sound. I didn't want to shout at whoever was lurking on my property because Heather was asleep and I didn't want to scare her.

The doors and windows were all locked. I just checked them. I wasn't about to go out there to confront whoever was looking into my daughter's bedroom.

Something hissed and kept hissing in

my room. I went back in there and was confronted by loud white noise that dominated my vision, assaulted my ears with its constant hissing. I turned off the TV and watched it, waiting for it to turn itself on again. It didn't.

There was no going back to sleep now. I grabbed a chair from the dining room and watched Heather sleep with the gun in my hand, keeping an eye on the window.

When the sun came up, Heather stirred, stretched, yawned and turned over. She opened her eyes and saw me and smiled that sweet little smile of hers.

"Good morning, Daddy."

"Good morning, sweetie. How was your sleep?"

"Good."

"That's good." I nodded slowly, stealing one final, paranoid glance at the window. "That's very good."

I made her breakfast. She sat down to watch cartoons and eat her Cheerios in front of the TV where her mom had been raped. Heather liked the new carpet. The other one was unsalvageable. Too much blood.

BODYCAM

But she didn't know that. She never will.

While Heather was distracted, I checked the mailbox and found a package. It was rectangular, crudely wrapped in newspaper. I looked around at the other houses, spaced apart by trees. We lived in the woods of Oro-Medonte, Ontario. You couldn't see any of the other houses from my windows at night because of all the trees. I was still carrying the gun in the pocket of my somewhat loose-fitting pajama pants. It thumped against my thigh with every step.

Inside, I tore the newspaper and found a videotape. There was a photograph of the front of the house on it serving as some kind of crude, homemade label. There were no notes pertaining to the contents of the videotape. It was just a videotape. Truthfully, I felt uneasy about holding it, studying the photograph, which was clearly taken from the end of the driveway. I left it in one of the upper cupboards where Heather couldn't reach. I double-checked the newspaper for a possible return address, but of course I didn't find one. Guess it was too much to ask for. I crumpled the newspaper and threw it in the garbage.

I returned to my room and for a second I saw Elaine sitting in front of the TV, leaning against the foot of the bed.

No. Not Elaine. *Heather*. God, she looked just like her mom. She wasn't eating anymore but I didn't see a bowl or a spoon anywhere. I asked her where it was. She said it was in the kitchen sink. I checked—there it was, just like she said, with the spoon still in it, full of tap water. Good girl.

I wanted to see Elaine. I didn't think Heather was ready to see her mom in that state just yet.

God. I just wanted to die. What kind of father would I be to subject her to that kinda sight? That would be the worst goddamn thing in the world.

Heather wanted help with puzzles later, so I helped her find all the right places to make the bunnies and the Thomas Kinkade cottages whole again. Lunchtime rolled around. I made her grilled cheese, which we ate together on the backyard patio. The trees behind the white picket

BODYCAM

fence rustled noisily as the spring breeze swept through their foliage.

Later, we played hide-and-seek. It took me fifteen minutes to find her hiding under the bathroom sink. It would've taken me longer if her giggling hadn't given her away.

Pastor Clemens visited later. Elaine read a *Winnie the Pooh* storybook in her room while I spoke with Clemens about a variety of things.

"Coffee?"

"If you're making some. If not, don't worry about it."

"I'm always making some, Lawrence."

"Rough nights?"

"Just can't sleep."

"I see. Everything else alright?"

"As opposed to what? Everything else being worse?"

He hesitated, as if searching for the right words. Before he could say something, I asked, "How do you like your coffee?"

"Black, thank you." I filled a white mug with java and handed it to him.

ALEXANDER ENGEL-HODGKINSON

"Thank you."

I sat across from him with my… fifth, perhaps sixth cup of the day.

"I'm sorry," he said.

"What for? I know you meant well. *I'm* the one who's sorry. Just, uh… just a little on edge these days, you know?"

He nodded. "I can't even pretend to imagine what that feels like…"

"You have any coyotes where you live?"

"Coyotes? No. Not that I've seen. Then again, I live in town. Why do you ask?"

"Just wondering. Thought I heard some this morning."

"Well, summer's just around the corner."

"True."

"Thinking about hunting them?"

"I only have a .38."

".38?"

"Yeah. Not exactly an ideal tool for hunting."

"A pistol? No." He chuckled. "No, it wouldn't be."

"A revolver, actually."

BODYCAM

"Oh, yeah? What kind?"

"Smith & Wesson Model 12.   I mainly got it for home defense." Thoughts of Elaine were creeping back. I sipped my coffee. "Lot of good that did for us…"

Clemens watched me sadly. I could tell he had trouble with these kinds of things. It was the thought that counted in my mind. I was glad he was here.

As he spoke about other things, my mind began to wander. I stared at the cupboards where I'd stashed the videotape until Clemens said something about the Andersons.

"What? I'm sorry, could you repeat that? I think I zoned out there. I'm sorry, you came all this way…"

"Ah, don't sweat the small stuff." He waved it off. "The Anderson boy asked about you."

"The Anderson boy… asked about me?"

"Well… he asked about the both of you."

What did he say, exactly?"

Clemens shrugged. "He simply asked about you guys, nothing more. Literally asked why you two weren't coming to church anymore."

"Between you and me?"

"Sure."

"I don't like that boy. I don't like anyone in that family. They're creepy, stuck-up pricks."

To my surprise, Clemens laughed, as if he knew that for a fact, like it was some obvious piece of knowledge. "While we're off the record, here, *no one* likes them, myself included."

"Really."

"They're a strange bunch, flaunting their wealth and status around, firmly conservative, and overbearing. The Petersons and the Cavanaughs have stopped coming to church, stopped answering my calls. The strange thing is, a week later, their daughter was reported missing. I remember *specifically* that the Anderson boy had been talking to the Cavanaugh girl the last Sunday I saw the Cavanaughs. She looked... uncomfortable, for lack of a better word, to be near him. Now, you know me. You know I asked everyone how they're doing. So that's what I did, I played that up in my approach. Because, let me tell you, she looked *really* uncomfortable. I asked them both how they enjoyed the service and that seemed to make the Anderson boy uncomfortable. His face was a little flushed, and the Cavanaugh girl left without a word, which was unlike her. She used to be quite chipper and talkative. You remember that?"

"Yeah, I remember. She was always bubbly whenever I saw her. I'll admit, I didn't pay much attention to anyone else. I wasn't religious. I never was. I'm definitely not religious now. I went because Elaine was. Elaine wanted to go, so I went. You know how it is. Or maybe you don't."

"Hey, when I was a kid, I didn't want to go to church, either. My parents made me. I hated it, especially when I was a teenager. When I had a child of my own, I couldn't think of it as anything other than a miracle." He slapped his chest lightly, with pride. "A born-again man sits before you now."

"Is your kid all grown up? Moved out? I'm sorry, maybe I just wasn't paying attention…" I faltered. The look on his face, as subdued as he tried to be, told me everything I needed to know. "Oh…"

"Hey, you couldn't have known."

"What happened, if… you don't mind me asking?"

"Drunk driver. He, uh, T-boned the car on Andrea's side. Timmy was in the back. He got the worst of it. He was one year old. Almost two." I stared at him, trying to get the words "I'm sorry" out, but he kept moving his mouth like he was going to say something. Eventually, he did. "We tried again, a few times, but the accident… well, it caused some internal damage. She can't have kids now."

"I'm sorry, Lawrence."

"Don't, don't be. We're thinking of adopting. There are lots of lonely kids out there. Kids who're sad and angry and completely alone. If we can't have any of our own, we figure maybe God wanted us to look elsewhere."

"Strange way of putting it."

"Yeah, I guess so." He forced a small laugh, but it was a very awkward, sputtering thing. "Anyway, uh, still between you and me?"

"It's not like any of this is on record," I joked. "I don't talk to many people, anyway. Just you, Heather, and Heather's teachers. That's about it. Oh, and whoever's working the till at the grocery store when I pass through. You get my point."

"True! True. Well." He seemed to be making his mind up about something. He sipped his coffee and sat for a few seconds. "I made an unannounced visit here today *because* of the Cavanaughs and the Petersons. I was concerned by all the absences lately, and I was worried that a phone call would... uh, give you fair warning to pretend you weren't home. Like it did them. I visited each place twice when they didn't return my calls. No one answered. I'm not sure what's going on." He sighed. "I'm sorry. I know it's improper to just show up unannounced..."

I shook my head. "Don't be. I get it. You're always welcome to visit anytime you like. I just decided I didn't want to come the church anymore. Like I said, that was Elaine's thing, not mine, and with

ALEXANDER ENGEL-HODGKINSON

Elaine gone…"

"I understand."

"And that Anderson boy."

"Yes. I understand perfectly."

We talked about a few other things and I offered to make him lunch, as the smell of grilled cheese still lingered in the kitchen, but he politely refused and went on his way, leaving another business card on the table.

In the evening, I made Heather some pizza and then I put her to bed and she fell asleep to a *Berenstein Bears* story.

I waited an hour. Then I retrieved the videotape from the cupboard. In my room, with the door closed, I pushed the tape into the VCR and sat on the foot of the bed, turning the TV's volume down to ten. At first, there was nothing but static. Then there was this deep, ambient noise and a black screen. A blue dot appeared in the center. It slowly expanded, its edges pointing out in four directions until it was a square, and this square came closer. I noticed there was something trapped within its borders, but the quality was poor. I could only see blotches of blue, pink, and

BODYCAM

purple. As it got closer still, the shapes became more pronounced, taking the form of a woman, lithe and tall, sitting in front of the screen in a translucent purple nightgown with frilly edges, which I distinctly remembered buying her for Valentine's Day seven years ago.

Elaine!

She was asleep, slumped against the foot of the bed, legs coiled delicately to one side across the old carpet. I watched, frozen, as the blackness around the square seeped into it like oil leaking through invisible cracks, and swirled round and round toward her. She was unaware of its presence, whatever *it* was. What was I looking at? I shouted at her to wake up! And she did, jolting awake as if she could hear me through the screen, but it was too late. The oily tendrils ensnared her, fastening her arms to the foot of the bed. She kicked out, tried to scream before one of its tentacles or limbs or whatever the hell they were, plunged down her throat. She gagged, eyes wide with terror, tears streaming down her face. And I jumped off the bed, pressed my palms against the screen, shouting her name.

Elaine! Elaine! Elaine!

All the while more black tendrils, simultaneously liquid and solid, swirled around her body beneath the nightgown. I could see their obscene, slimy wet black skin gleaming in the TV's blue glow under the thin fabric of her nightgown before it was torn off her body. I screamed for this shapeless thing to get the hell away from her. I screamed helplessly, tears welling up in my eyes as I watched the tendril in her mouth fatten and pulsate. I saw it bulging in her throat, and then she writhed, legs convulsing, arms and fingers rigid as the tendril slithered further down inside her. Her chest puffed out, her back arched, and I saw its end emerge from beneath her. More shapeless matter consumed her legs and forced them open, exposing her to the screen, whatever was doing this, the thing behind the lens, as the tendril curled upward and violently penetrated her. Her eyes bulged. I heard her gargled scream. I heard her choke, and fearfully whimper, and I cried and wailed, shaking the TV set until I nearly pulled it off the stand. Her

BODYCAM

arms and legs stretched and curled in spirals like strands of melted rubber. Her bones crumbled, crackling so loud it hurt my ears. I could hear her screams intensify, filling the room like a siren, shaking the walls, the floor...

Then they lifted her, lifted her off the floor, her arms and head and torso rotating to the left, her legs and full, oozing orifices gyrating to the right. I howled, I begged, I pleaded—

She didn't snap in half. Didn't break apart. She simply stretched and stretched across the room as the thing filled her insides, her skin distending as things bulged from within. Holes started to slide open like eyelids, but there weren't eyes behind those eyelids, just things that looked like human snakes with ten eyes and four faces slinking out from tiny openings. They slapped wetly on the floor, covered in slime the colour of blood—maybe it *was* blood. They shrieked helplessly on the rug, their mouths widening, their faces becoming broad and then fusing all together, becoming their own shapeless patchwork of faces that mimicked Heather's.

ALEXANDER ENGEL-HODGKINSON

Elaine split down the middle and yawned open, revealing a deep, black void within her—

I tore the tape out of the VCR but before I could throw it I collapsed on my knees and vomited and passed out.

It'd been hours before I came to, and when it all came back to me what I was doing, what I saw, I bolted for the phone and called the police.

I could barely form a coherent sentence every time they asked me to describe as best I could what I saw on the tape. I told them to see for themselves. So they kept me in the kitchen, trying to talk me down as I sipped gingerly from a glass of scotch, while a trio of officers reviewed the tape in my room. I apologized for the vomit on the floor. They told me not to worry about it. The officers were as quiet as they could, and kept the bedroom door shut for the benefit of my sleeping daughter in the next room. How she slept through all my screaming I'll never be able to figure out. She used to be a light sleeper. I had another officer check in on her. She was fine, sleeping like an angel.

BODYCAM

They came out a few minutes later and said the tape was blank. I wanted to scream. How could it be blank? After what I *saw*, how the hell could it be fucking blank?! I told them to take it away, just take it, get it out of this house.

They did that much, at least.

FRIDAY/MAY 9TH/1997
AM 00:03:23:40

I awoke in a cold sweat and it was just like the day I received that tape; I felt chills like I was waking up in the Antarctic. Felt like I was freezing, but it was hot outside. It was a humid morning. I had the fan blowing; lot of good it did me. Cheap garbage.

Images from that tape were flashing through my mind. The visualization of her face distended in agony was seared into my brain and I couldn't get her likeness out from behind my eyelids. I started seeing things and the shadows on the walls played tricks on me. I could see her face slice across the wall every time a car drove by outside, their headlights streaking in the form of her terrified face, her eyes wide and mouth agape as they must have been when she first saw him.

It was like I could still hear that scream in the distance. I couldn't shake her shrieks out of my ears. Just kept echoing again and again. I knew it was only the coyotes lurking in the trees behind the house, baying at the moon.

36

BODYCAM

I had to be sure.

Taking the loaded .38 snubnose out of the drawer of the bedside table (I'd since moved it from the dresser on the other side of the room), I crept through the house, from my room at the end of the hall to the bathroom on my right, then Heather's room on my left. I watched her for a moment, listened to her soft breathing, the sheets rising and falling gently. I left her door open as I went through the rest of the house, exiting the hall into the kitchen and dining room, then the living room at the other end of the house. I peered through the curtains, opened the screen door, and turned on the patio light for a look into the backyard, but it was empty. I looked out as far as I could across the backyard, into the impenetrable darkness of the forest on the other side. I turned off the patio light and checked the handle. Locked. I turned around, crossed the living room to the door leading into the basement. It wasn't completely finished; cold, damp, its walls and floor dusty concrete. The washer and dryer were down here. I turned on the light and descended the wooden stairs, each step creaking loudly under my weight. I had a brief look around. It was empty, with no places to hide. Just a cupboard where the detergents and fabric softeners were stored, along with some cleaning products; the washer, the dryer, and a foldable drying rack. There wasn't even a window down here.

I went back upstairs and returned to Heather's room, deciding I'd watch her sleep for a while. I glanced at the window and the person outside stared back in at me. In the next instant he was gone, and so was I. I snatched the house key off the rack and the flashlight out of the drawer closest to the kitchen sink before I stepped out onto the front porch, turning only to lock the front door behind me. I pocketed the key, turned on the flashlight, and listened for the sound of feet padding on the grass. I heard the wind blowing through the trees, the leaves rustling, sounding like rushing water above me. I ran around back, flashlight probing every inch of darkness as I jogged, and just as I'd reached the backyard a shape disappeared into the forest. I bolted across the yard to the edge of the forest, my

BODYCAM

flashlight beam slicing through the dark. I could hear someone moving around in there. Twigs snapped under running feet, foliage rustling, shoes scraping on tree roots. The thicket was just too goddamned dense to see who was in there.

I shouted after them. "Who's out there? If I see you again, you're dead, you understand? I'm armed! Next time I put a bullet in your goddamned face! Leave us alone! Do you hear me? *Leave us alone!*"

The forest fell silent. Everything was still. Even the breeze had stopped. So I went back inside and double-checked all the locks. I set the key on the hook, a little round yellow ornament with red hair and a sinister grin painted on it dangling from its chain. I left the flashlight on the counter next to the coffee maker. I returned to Heather's room.

Elaine sat on the edge of her bed, gently stroking her fingers through Heather's hair as she slept. Elaine was naked, her skin ashen and covered with stretch marks. My voice caught in my throat as I stared at her, and then she turned to look at me. She froze. Her arms were suddenly twice as long as they should have been. When she stood up, I noticed her legs were long, too. Long and spindly. She towered above me and shuddered. Her eyes were penetrating discs, her pupils dilated in an unreadable expression. Hate? Pain? Joy? Love? Fear? It seemed like all of them and none of them at once. I couldn't move. I was numb with fear. A violent tingle in the back of my skull kept me immobilized. It didn't seem real. She didn't seem real. Yet my eyes tracked the slightest movements she made, the little jolts and muscle spasms. Every movement was janky and unnatural. She didn't... seem *real*. She went down on all fours, her limbs like a spider's legs, and her neck stretched back, as if her spine was suddenly capable of arching upwards away from her shoulders. Those eyes never left me as she crawled toward me slowly, methodically. The sudden advance made me stagger out of the room. Instinctively I raised the gun and pointed it at her. Elaine's expression didn't change. It was still an indecipherable mask of hate, love, fear, pain, and joy as she drew closer and closer.

BODYCAM

I stumbled toward the kitchen and her head floated out of Heather's room on its long neck and she wouldn't stop staring at me, wouldn't even blink, as her distorted body scurried into my bedroom. Her face followed it and I followed the face in a horrified daze.

I stood in the doorway as her body hovered between her four spidery legs toward the TV set, which turned itself on, as if activated by her close proximity. She shrank down.

"E-Elaine...?"

She crawled inside the TV. "Elaine!" I was frightened by what I was seeing. Her foot disappeared through the screen. I scrambled along the side of the bed and touched the screen, but it was just a screen. The barrier was up once more. My fingers slid down the glass as it faded to black. I began to cry.

Hours later, I managed to hold it together until the school bus picked up Heather. I noticed as she was boarding the bus that the flag on the mailbox was up. When she was out of sight, I checked the mailbox.

ALEXANDER ENGEL-HODGKINSON

A rectangular object wrapped crudely in newspaper. I knew before I held it in my hand that it was another videotape. I wanted to call the police, but all they saw was a blank videotape. I showed them the exact one—it was still in the VCR. They should've seen what I saw. If only they could! I didn't understand why they couldn't, but I knew that calling them again wasn't gonna do me much good.

Like before, there was a photograph in the place of a label, no return addresses, no traces of where it'd come from. The photograph was different—this one was taken from the house's west side, from behind one of the pine trees by the ditch. So... I pushed it into the VCR. I made sure it was at the beginning. Then I pushed play.

The screen was soft, fuzzy colours and cheerful synth-pop music as the camera zoomed out of a blonde woman's smiling face. It took me a few seconds to realize why she looked so familiar—Donna Anderson from a past decade. Her hairstyle was the same as it was now, but her face was more youthful, her smile devoid of the

BODYCAM

condescension and malice I was used to seeing. She had a nice smile, and her body had never looked better than it did in this video, clad in a skin-tight aerobics leotard with a bright blue unzipped motorcycle jacket draped over her shoulders.

Confused, I watched her gesture towards a group of colourfully dressed people behind her congregated around what looked like a bronze statue of a man with a Macintosh monitor for a head and a keyboard across his burly chest. She was reading off a list of questions about what the viewer knows about transhumanism, human evolution, its correlation with the Christian faith, and if the viewer ever considered the possibility that science and spiritual faith can co-exist. And then she said something about coming down to a resort, but the audio cut out when she said the name of the place. She spread her arms out as a phone number appeared and told the viewer to call that number. I read it aloud several times as I searched around for a pen and paper. Bedside table. Top drawer. I scribbled the number down, and then I heard Donna say to me—to *me*—that she knew I'd been staring at her tits all that time.

I did a double-take, startled. The music had stopped. The camera was no longer panning over the lustrous grounds of some mythical resort. Now it was stationary, and Donna was standing in the center of the screen glaring at me with her fists on her hips. She seemed almost pleased as she tore the leotard off her body, exposing herself, bending down and hooking her fingers between her legs. She moaned, asking me if I wanted to fuck her, fuck her hard, fuck her like I hated her, and I answered no. I realized I was talking to my TV. I was… talking to Donna on my TV. I would have felt ridiculous if her seductive glare contorted into a shriveled, demonic mask of hate. She slid her fingers across her breasts, shuddering violently as her fingers brushed her nipples, and she dug her fingers into her flesh and tore a rift in her center. She shed her flesh like it was a bathrobe, the way a lover disrobes for their significant other at the start of a night of passion. I watched her pumping heart turn black behind her ribcage. The heart shifted around within her, growing larger, taking the shape of a woman curled in the fetal position. Donna moaned as she fondled her flaccid breasts as the woman inside her screamed. It was Elaine screaming, imprisoned within Donna's ribs, reaching out for me. Donna spoke again, but it was Elaine's voice coming out of her mouth, much louder than the Elaine screaming in its cage, and she asked if I wanted her or not. Make your decision, goddamn you.

I asked her—*it*—what it wanted from me. What the fuck did it want from me?!

Donna dropped her flesh coat on the floor and stood rigidly. Her face melted. Eyes without lids burned into my retinas, immobilized me. Liquid flesh dribbled over her skeleton, over the imprisoned Elaine, muffling her cries. The amount of pasty-white liquid flesh cascading from her skull seemed to be infinite. Pink muscle tissue slithered and throbbed in overlapping layers. When her entire skeleton was covered in it, the flesh began to take on a new form. Elaine's form, down to the smallest detail. Her hair sprouted rapidly from her scalp and formed the bangs that had always framed her delicate face.

She sat down and opened her legs in front of a pitch black background and told me to come to her. Arms outstretched, she called out to me again. She wouldn't stop saying my name.

I turned off the TV. I took out the tape. It felt hot in my palm. I carried it with me as I took a match and some newspaper into the backyard and I threw the tape into the fire pit enclosed by old bricks. I covered it with newspaper and started a fire. I made several trips through the screen door, gathering every videotape I could find, and dumping the tapes into the fire pit, occasionally feeding it with gasoline. I watched the film shrivel and melt in the heat as the plastic cases cracked and popped open. Four boxes of tapes—family memories, Hollywood blockbusters, TV recordings—all burned that day.

I'd hoped that would be the end of it. I silently prayed to a God I didn't believe in, any god that was listening, that no more tapes would arrive.

Heather came home at four, stepping off the bus. She came inside just as I'd

BODYCAM

poured my fifth scotch for the afternoon. I was in no shape to cook, no mood to help her with her homework, and I had no motivation to do anything with her. She asked if I was okay. I told her daddy's feeling a little drained.

Drained. A gross understatement. After burning the tapes, there was a horrible smell that lingered in the air. Not like the toxic stench of burning plastic, but of something more... organic. Something that was once alive. I'd showered since then but it was still there, clinging to me persistently. Heather asked about the smell. I told her not to worry about it; it would go away soon.

It didn't go away, and the tapes kept coming.

SUNDAY/JULY 6TH/1997
AM 00:03:33:34

I woke up with a start from someone shouting at the foot of my bed. I tumbled out of bed and hit the floor, eyes darting to the static snow on the TV screen, shifting in weird black-and-white patterns. A voice was saying something urgently, but it was too distorted; there was too much interference in the broadcast, if it was a broadcast, to make out what they were saying. I couldn't even tell if it was a man or a woman speaking. I saw a shock of blonde hair on the screen, distorted, stretched horizontally in a grotesque smear, before the screen panned downward over a fuzzy patchwork of pubic hair and faces.

I played the latest tape again. The photograph on it had been taken from behind the house. Heather's bedroom window was focused in the very center.

In the video, the POV was getting closer to the square that framed Elaine's figure as she watched from afar, like she was observing my slow, methodical approach. She didn't seem scared this time. There was something different in her eyes.

48

BODYCAM

She wore the same seductive look she gave me every time we put Heather to bed, during our most private moments. Our most intimate moments. She wanted me.

As the camera drew closer, so did she. Reaching out, touching the screen, I looked down and saw the swell of her naked breasts. Her tanned skin glistened under harsh lights I couldn't see, glowing golden brown. My eyes drifted further downward, over her flat stomach across the neatly trimmed tufts of hair between her shapely legs to her toes. She said my name and I looked back into her eyes, into that seductive gaze that held me in place. She reached down. Touched me. I shuddered. She felt so real. Like she was there. I blinked and suddenly I was swelling in her mouth and I could feel myself enclosed, her tongue swirling around me, tasting me, taking all of me into her throat and even further still. So warm... so wet and... yes... just like that... you remembered how I like it.

I watched her head bob up and down in my lap. I moaned, feeling a jolt as she focused on pleasuring the head. I ran my fingers through her hair, easing into it, feeling it coming. My hand sank into her doughy skull. Alarmed, I saw her face had melted into a puddle of eyes that oozed across my abdomen and I screamed as this throbbing substance extending through the TV screen poured over me. It was thick, flesh-like, yet liquid at the same time. It was warm—*hot*. It was hot. It was not my wife but it sounded like her, it *felt* like her. It was covered in *her* eyes, all giving me that seductive look, their lids half-closed over the palest green I'd ever seen.

I screamed again. I threw my hands on it, slapped it, punched it, each point of impact transforming into her sex, and every time I hit it the thing shuddered with obscene pleasure and I couldn't stop screaming as this thing had its way with me. It felt like Elaine. The soft skin of her legs slick with sweat as they enclosed around me. Her nails digging slightly into me every time I thrust further inside her. Her breath hot and ragged, prickling my skin.

It sounded like Elaine. Those muffled cries she made when she finished

BODYCAM

on top of me, trying her best to keep from waking Heather in the next room. I felt her tighten around me as she came, hot liquid splashing my abdomen.

I tried to crawl away but the bed was in the way and I couldn't climb onto it because the creature kept me glued to the goddamn floor. I didn't want to feel good anymore. I didn't *feel* good! I was being raped by an obscene imitation of my nightmares. It was shaped like a cock, its flesh shriveled, resembling gills, covered in her eyes and a dozen leaking vaginal orifices. It was sucking me in. I couldn't feel my legs; it was sucking me all the way inside of it. Below my waist had been totally consumed. I could feel my pants dissolving, my cock hard and swollen as the thing's slippery innards tightened and stirred and pulsated around me. Rough yet soft, warm, tight and wet, so *wet*... she was soaked...

I felt her fingers probing me from behind, two at first, then more wriggled in and I struggled against the overwhelming sensations, my pelvis burning, my testicles aching, white-hot fire, as it forced me to cum. I felt the entire fleshy mass bubble pleasurably; I heard four mouths moaning in my ears with overlapping, orgasmic bliss. It wouldn't stop. It squeezed harder, painfully, punishing me as the mouths whispered, trying to coax me into fucking it all night long.

Its back split open, and she sprouted like a flower from its depths, covered in a filmy white substance with a faintly blue sheen, the TV screen bright blue behind her. Her face was redder now, her chest heaving, her breathing heavy as she reached out to me. Framed my tear-streaked face in her hands and stared into my eyes.

"It's okay, baby. Just a little longer," she moaned. "Just a little more!"

No!

The vibrations became more aggressive and I was trapped, helplessly watching her rock back and forth, squeezing me so hard I felt like I was going to burst. My muscles screamed. My bones ached. The mouths were sucking on me like leeches. My fingers were being suctioned into her sexual orifices, flaps of writhing flesh tickling my fingers as they

BODYCAM

sank into her. Felt just like her, every one of them. Our dates when I'd sneak a finger into her panties as I drove her home after our date. She squirmed in her seat, her hand gripping my arm as she thrust my fingers deeper. I curved them. She opened her mouth and gasped, nails digging into my arm, and just when she was about to cum I felt her thighs suddenly crush my fingers. She demanded I pull over to the side of the road and take her in the back seat. I obeyed, heart pounding. My whole body was trembling so much I could barely keep my foot from accidentally flooring the gas. I put it in park. She giggled as she dived between the front seats into the back. I crawled after her, smacking her backside playfully, and I hovered over her, smelling her sweat. I kissed her. I tore off her clothes. I wanted her so bad. I couldn't get enough of her. She lay there, completely naked, her fingers dragging my pants and underwear down. She gripped me tightly in her delicate hands. She was already so wet and horny that foreplay wasn't needed. We were too impatient for foreplay, anyway. We needed each other desperately, so I spread her legs and plunged deep inside her…

"No!"

I trembled violently as I felt the thing's members wriggling around in my ass, stretching me painfully, and it wouldn't stop. I couldn't get free. The white-hot intensity returned; needles in my brain and my crotch simultaneously as she forced me to cum in her again. The backseat was damp now… now… the floor… I was… she was…

Heather screamed at me and I saw her in the doorway as my semen splashed across the glowing TV screen. I stood naked on my knees, my cock enclosed in my fists. She stood in her pajamas, half hidden behind the frame, watching me in wide-eyed terror. I stared at her in shock. I said her name. I reached out to her and she screamed and ran away. I heard her bedroom door slam shut.

I looked at my fingers, mired in my seed. I whirled around and around, searching for the monster. The TV was a blank blue screen. Elaine was nowhere to be found. It was just me in here, the skin

BODYCAM

on my cock rubbed red and sore, my fingers stinging from the constant friction.

I fell against my semen-streaked TV and howled in what must've been some kind of psychotic release, as strands of the stuff dripped onto the floor. My entire body trembled with intense rage and agony and terror and God that fucking *stench* what was it?! I couldn't keep my emotions bottled anymore. Soon I was thrashing around, smashing through the tiers on the bookshelf, books and trinkets cascading to the floor; I swiped the framed pictures off the dresser; I picked up the VCR and shook it but I couldn't bring myself to smash the goddamned thing like I knew I should've because deep down I knew Elaine was still in there somewhere.

I took a shower and sobbed uncontrollably under scalding water, scrubbing my skin until I bled in places. I still didn't feel clean. Why? Why was this happening to me? Why Elaine? Why her? I couldn't stop screaming it. Why? Why? I beat the shower walls with my fists until my knuckles bled and then I kept on pounding them on the white tiles, smashing them. Why? Why? Why? Jagged porcelain biting into my flesh, slicing my skin, needling my hands. Why? Why? Why? Why? My bloody hands resembled chunks of red pulp, clenched so tightly I wasn't sure I could unclench them anymore. I could only scream and cry as my blood streaked across the shower curtain and the cracked walls. I slipped and fell in the tub and the last thing I remember is waking up to the phone ringing. By then the sun was shining through the small square pane of frosted glass. The water was still spraying over me, freezing cold. I was shivering. Felt raw to the bone. My hide felt numb and leathery.

The phone.

I crawled out of the tub and shut the water off. My hands throbbed. They were still clenched balls of crimson, gnarly skin tatters. My head spun. Woozy, I fell against the walls and used them to keep myself on my feet. Follow the phone. I followed it, drawn to its shrill, electronic beeping that seemed to echo through the whole house.

The phone. I threw myself on the

counter and dragged the receiver off the cradle. I put it to my ear. Someone, a voice, distant and hollow, said, "She's a sinner."

"Who?"

"That filthy whore, that temptress."

"*Who*?!"

"The filthy whore. The temptress. The slut who led me astray."

I dropped the phone.

"Who…?"

Hours later, I came to on the kitchen floor and realized that Heather was standing over me, staring down at me over Marley's head. She hugged him tightly against her chest. Marley looked down on me with condescending googly eyes. Goddamn bear.

Heather asked me if I was okay. I looked down and saw my bloody fists. I noticed Heather had covered me with a blanket and even tucked a pillow behind my head. My neck ached from sleeping while sitting against the cupboard. She asked again if I was okay. She started to cry, and asked again if I was going to be okay through her tears.

I shushed her gently. I told her everything would be alright. Nothing was going to happen to her. Daddy just had a bad night. A really bad night. I'm sorry you had to see what you did. I'm sorry.

She said it was okay. I knew it wasn't.

Keeping the blanket around me, I made my way into the bathroom. Heather offered her shoulder to lean on, though it was hardly any help at all. I appreciated the thought and played along. I unhitched the showerhead from its hook and sat down on the edge of the tub. I gave it to Heather and held out my hands. She sprayed a few layers of caked blood off. While she rummaged through the drawers, I picked a few loose flaps of skin from my cuts. She came back with a box of Band-Aids with dinosaurs on them and tenderly applied lots of Band-Aids to every cut she saw. I could barely move my fingers now; she must've used thirty, at least. I had to laugh at that, and when she scolded me for harming myself, it was like Elaine had shrunk herself down and was doing her best to

BODYCAM

sound authoritative and intimidating while waggling a forefinger at me in complete disapproval. I laughed a little harder. It'd been a long time since I laughed. My reaction made her pout. She reminded me that she was super serious, and that if I do it again, I'll be in big trouble.

I hugged her tight. It took everything in me not to burst into tears.

I got dressed, swallowed a few painkillers to numb the pain in my hands, legs, and prostate, and made her some pancakes for brunch. Despite her apparent forgiveness, I still couldn't look her in the eye. I was so mortified. I never felt so helplessly ashamed of myself. Was it really my fault, or did I lose control? Maybe I had none to begin with. I couldn't accept that. Not after what my daughter saw. No daughter should ever see... *that*.

Was that what Elaine suffered? Is that why she reverted to a hollow shell? Christ, something like that... something like *that*, I could never have fucking imagined. I saw the pain on her face, the horror. It's enough to drive anyone over the brink of sanity. I didn't think I was too far behind.

Heather helped me clean up the broken tiles and wipe my blood out of the tub and off the shower walls. I did the curtains, because those were a bitch to do, and I had her wear gardening gloves before handling the porcelain. After we cleaned up the bathroom, I carried the VCR outside and took a bat to it until the machine and the tape inside it were reduced to a heap of crinkled black tape and plastic fragments. Then I set fire to it all with some gasoline in the fire pit. Heather and I sat there and watched it burn for a while.

To my shock and confusion, Donna Anderson came knocking sometime in the early evening. When I opened the door I damn-near slammed it in her face. But she wasn't smiling that condescending smile. Her eyes were glazed and had dark rings under them. She knew what I was going to do, and said one word before I could do it.

"Please."

It sounded desperate, sincere, and fearful all at once. As if this was it. Her last resort. I couldn't quite put it into words, but whatever it was, there was something in her voice and the timid way she carried herself that convinced me to at least listen to what she had to say for a minute.

What the hell do you want?" I paused as more questions sprang to mind. "How do you know where I live? Did Clemens give you my address?"

"No."

"Then how...?"

"I need to talk to you."

"Oh, really."

"Look, I wouldn't be here if I had any other option." I stood in the doorway, staring at her expectantly. "I delivered the tapes."

I bristled. Furious heat seemed to surge through me. My muscles tensed. I stepped out onto the porch and closed the door between myself and Heather. I said to Donna, very quietly, through gritted teeth, "You'd better have a good explanation, or I'll draw. I'll put a bullet through your fucking eye right on this porch." I had my hand tucked in my housecoat, pretending the revolver was in my pocket. The gun was in the house.

ALEXANDER ENGEL-HODGKINSON

She glanced down, then back up. "You have a gun?"

I nodded. ".38. Talk."

She was a wreck. She looked like she'd just tumbled off a four-month cocaine binge and clearly hadn't slept for days. Her appearance was haggard, her movements jumpy. She was afflicted with a high level of nervous clumsiness I'd ever seen. Usually she was calm, collected, cold, the works; but here? Here was a day I never thought I'd see.

"I was forced to do it."

"Bullshit."

"It's true."

"Bull. Shit."

"I didn't have a choice. I... I was petrified. I had no control. Ever since '82, I did my damnedest to avoid those people but... but *it* had always been there. Possessing me. Watching me."

"What people?" I asked. "What were they doing?"

She shook her head, blinking back tears. She wouldn't say.

Or wouldn't.

"Talk to me, Donna.

BODYCAM

"It found us." Her voice sounded small and far away. "*It* found *me*. It would never let me go. I can never leave, even if I left. It's in my home now. It found me." She started to blubber. "It's in my goddamn *home* and now that it's in, it won't stop until it gets what it wants."

"Who? What? What the hell are you talking about?"

"Shoot me."

"What? Are you crazy?"

"No. Not yet. Shoot me. Please."

"What is 'it,' Donna?"

"Shoot me. Shoot me."

"Donna—"

"*Shoot* me!" She smacked her palm across her forehead. "Right here! Shoot me in the head! Here! *Here!*"

"I'm not shooting you. What the hell is wrong with you?"

"Shoot me! Shoot me and get out! And take that little bitch with you!"

"Hey!"

"Shoot me!" She lunged for my pocket. I jumped away and shoved her off the porch.

"Get off my property!"

ALEXANDER ENGEL-HODGKINSON

She leaped up off the gravel, arms stretched toward the sky. "Do it! I'm right here! I'm ready to die! Shoot me!" She tittered and guffawed. She choked on her tears, swinging from maniacal glee to absolute fear and back again. I wanted to go back inside and lock the door. I wished I hadn't left the gun in my bedroom.

But then she caught a glimpse of something by the side of the house and shrieked. It was the most startling, bloodcurdling thing I'd heard; it sounded exactly like the shouting that woke me this morning. Scared the shit out of me. I watched in shock as she begged whatever she saw not to take her, not like *that*. When I looked I didn't see anything except my car parked on the gravel lot. She stumbled and fell over herself back to her car, scrambling to get away from whatever it was she could see. "Leave!" she shrieked. "Leave and never come back! Leave me alone! Stay away from my family or I'll kill you, too!"

Then she was gone. I was left with a lot more questions than answers.

BODYCAM

SATURDAY/AUGUST 9TH/1997
AM 00:03:43:33

I hadn't been sleeping well. I sat flipping through channels, anxious for reasons I couldn't fathom. I had subscribed to cable since I'd thrown out the VCR, and I burned every videotape I received since then. Hell, I camped out, tried my damnedest to watch the mailbox and catch the sender in the act, but no one came until I'd dozed off. It was as if they knew when I was nodding off before they made their move, because the following morning I'd find another tape in the mailbox and then I'd burn it. Eventually the neighbours started complaining about the smell drifting through the trees into their yards, so I dug a large hole in the forest behind the house and started dumping the tapes in it.

I tried a few more times to catch the culprit. I camped out in my kitchen with an endless supply of coffee, but I kept fucking nodding off and they kept succeeding in getting away.

So I went to the electronics store and brought home a security camera, which of course came with state-of-the-art motion detection. The clerk said the camera would only record when its sensor detected motion in order to save film. I had to get blank videotapes and a VCR, which I was very uneasy about. I hooked up the VCR in my room, sandwiched between the cable box and the TV set, and left a blank tape in it, and used large staples to pin the surveillance cable along the trimmings on the walls and ceiling, all the way to the camera, which I'd mounted above the front door. It was pointed right at that mailbox. I'd tested it out, approaching its field of vision from different routes; the trees on either side, as well as the direct and shortest route from the front porch to the mailbox. I'd accidentally erased the first test when I rewound the footage, but once I got the hang of that, it worked out just fine. A timecode in the corner of the screen jumped between my appearances in its field of vision. I had Heather run out a few feet from the porch while I watched the TV screen, which was blank until she hopped off the porch. I called her back in and after about sixty seconds, the screen went blank again.

BODYCAM

It worked! It felt strange to see myself on my TV screen. I looked haggard, skinny, and a little old. I was barely forty, but I looked older. Guess it was all starting to wear me down. Too much coffee. Not enough sleep. Not enough food—well, *good* food. I made sure Heather ate nutritional meals, but I didn't really do much for myself anymore. I barely showered. Barely changed my clothes. I kept myself hydrated between pots of coffee with shots of whiskey and glasses of scotch.

When I set up the camera, I felt more excited than I had in months. I went to bed but I couldn't sleep. I stared down the length of the bed at the TV, on the surveillance channel, waiting for the picture to blink to life, waiting for that bastard to activate its motion sensor so I could catch him and end this once and for all. The mailbox was conveniently located under a cone of light from a roadside lamppost, so anyone who came near it would be illuminated. Oh, sure, they could come in a disguise, but I'd worry about that after the fact.

ALEXANDER ENGEL-HODGKINSON

I'd dozed off eventually, and came to about four hours later. The screen was still black. I went outside and checked the mailbox.

Another tape… the photograph was taken just a few feet away from my bedroom window. The curtains were always drawn—I'd bought curtains and venetian blinds for all the windows—so no one could look in, but we could look out.

I hurried back inside and checked the footage on the surveillance tape… but there *was* no footage! What the hell? I checked the VCR and found it empty and almost screamed at the top of my fucking lungs. Fuck! I could've sworn I put a tape in there! How could I have been so fucking stupid?! I almost shoved the whole VCR and cable box off the TV when I slapped a fresh tape into it. Then I took the tape that arrived outside, and crossed the backyard to about ten feet from the dark line of shrubs and hurled it into the approximate area where I'd dug out the hole with the other tapes in it.

And now, here I was, flipping through cable channels. Nothing but talk shows and

BODYCAM

skin flicks. I wasn't interested in them. The harsh glare of the screen was burning my eyes.

My head turned in the direction of a rapid succession of pounding on the front door. I grabbed the .38 and tucked it into my housecoat as I slipped into it, tied the sash around my waist as I entered the kitchen to the door next to the counter, and flicked on the front porch light.

It was Mr. Anderson. I couldn't remember his first name. His usual stoic expression was replaced by something manic and fearful. He wore a baseball cap, a sweatshirt, and loose-fitting jean shorts. When the porchlight came on, he flinched and stared at it with buggy eyes, and then leaned against the door, trying to peer through the curtain over the window in the door. I knew he couldn't see me because I stood next to the key rack beside the door, my back touching the end of the kitchen counter. His shadow darted around on the linoleum floor as he tried to get a good look inside. I asked him without opening the door, "What do you want?" I hoped Heather wouldn't wake up.

ALEXANDER ENGEL-HODGKINSON

"I need to speak to you."

"I can hear you just fine over here." I started when he tried the door, but it was locked.

"Please let me in. *Please*."

"Go away."

"I know you were the last person to speak to my wife."

"What's this about? Are you accusing me of... having *relations* with your wife? If that's what this is, you can just forget about it."

"I know you were the last person to speak to my wife. Let me in. I need to speak to you."

I didn't let him in. My hand was gripping the gun in my housecoat pocket. "Leave now."

"I know you were the last person to speak to my wife. Let me in. I need to speak to you, man to man."

I struggled to keep my voice calm. "That's not gonna happen. We can talk, if we really have to, but I'm not letting you into my house." Before I could ask him what exactly he wanted to know, he hurled himself into the door. The window pane above the kitchen sink rattled.

"Let me *in*, goddamn you."

"I have a gun, Anderson! If you continue to act threateningly, I'll be forced to use it."

He bounced his forehead against the window, spider-webbing the outer pane, as he yelled that he'd kill my whore, the whore that corrupted and destroyed his family; and then ran away into the trees. A few red spots glimmered within the cracks on the glass.

I didn't go back to sleep that morning. I decided to call the police, but the line was dead. I wondered if that son of a bitch cut the landline or if there was something wrong with the outlet. I tried a different outlet, but it was the same there, too. Shit.

I was seriously sick and tired of this family. These fucking people were crazy. First the wife, now the husband a month later. Next, their fucking sons will be picketing my yard or something.

Exasperated, I made myself some coffee and habitually searched the property through the windows for any sign of Mr. Anderson. I didn't see a car out there, and I didn't hear him leave in one. I didn't want to consult the surveillance tape in case I accidentally erased any important footage. I changed the input channel to the surveillance channel, but it was black. With the landline severed, I figured it was safe to assume that he was hiding somewhere, waiting for me to come out. Waiting for an opportunity to come in.

I sat down and tried to imagine every possible explanation to their raving bullshit. They called my wife a whore, which is something I'll never forgive them for. First Donna, now her husband. They'd said the same thing, said my wife ruined their family. How? How and why would she do that? Elaine would never do that. She wouldn't intentionally do anything to harm anyone else. She was sweet. She was gentle. She was *tolerant*. Sometimes she went over there to have social dinners with them. She always brought homemade apple crumble pie for dessert.

Was she having an affair with Mr. Anderson? I never noticed anything between them, but maybe that was because I actively avoided them whenever I could.

BODYCAM

No. Drive that thought out of your mind. Elaine would never do that. Elaine loved me. She loved Heather. She'd never have done that. But maybe Mr. Anderson *wanted* her to. Maybe she rejected him. Maybe he didn't like that. That would put a strain on any marriage, especially one as conservative and obsessed with image as the Andersons.

It didn't really matter in the present time. The main concern, right now, was keeping Anderson out of my house, and finding a way to get Heather safely off the property. The car was out front, making it highly likely that Mr. Anderson was camping out in the trees by the road outside of the camera's cone of vision. Our best hope was to run to the car, but there was always the possibility that Anderson had a firearm. I didn't want to risk that. Even if he wasn't armed, the trees were only fifteen feet away from the car—and the car was ten feet from the porch's steps.

There was also the possibility that he'd tampered with the car in some way— slashed the tires, disabled the engine, or something else. I hadn't parked it in view of the camera, which now made me curse my own lack of forethought.

No. We had better chances staying inside. I double-checked all the doors and windows to make sure they were locked, then I picked up Heather—bless her little soul, she didn't wake up as I carried her to my room. I tucked her into my bed and watched her sleep with Marley clutched close to her chest. She muttered in her sleep and dreamed on. I shut the bedroom door and sat at the foot of the bed with the gun in my right hand and the TV remote in my left. I switched back to the surveillance input channel but accidentally hit the down channel button. I was about to switch it back up when I glanced at the screen and, instead of static, I saw the side of the house—*my* side of the house. It took me a second to realize I'd somehow tapped into a separate camera's broadcast. But how? I thought closed-circuit television couldn't be accessed without an adjoining cord?

Yet here I was with the startling revelation that somebody had come up with a similar idea to my own. They had installed a camera in the trees. I tested the

BODYCAM

down button again and flipped to another view of the house from a different vantage point. Heather's window. I went down again, seeing the other side of the house; my spine tingling with icy fear as the creeping realization dawned on me: those photographs were screenshots with the timecodes cropped out. They'd been watching us the entire time.

I started trembling as the tingling fear intensified. I couldn't steady my hands. Cold sweat seeped from my pores, my clothes clung to me, and I shivered every time the small tabletop fan on the dresser blew its artificial breeze over me.

The timecode was constantly moving in the corner of the screen. I consulted the digital clock on the dresser, and after a few minutes I determined that the live feed from the other cameras was delayed by about twenty seconds.

I wished I had multiple TVs with the same hookup so that I could follow all the feeds at once without constantly flipping through channels. The only upside to this situation was that the house was built in the center of a clearing, surrounded by trees.

ALEXANDER ENGEL-HODGKINSON

Even if he could see the house from wherever he was hiding, I'd be able to see him coming from any direction.

There were eight cameras total. Two on each side, three behind the backyard, and one across the street pointed at the front. I tried to rewind the footage for the one stationed across the street, but I got the circle-backslash symbol instead.

Two hours passed without incident. My thumbs were tired from constantly flipping through all the vantage points. My body was feeling stiff from the way I'd been sitting for the past few hours. I started to reconsider making a run for the car, but the risk of it being disabled was still too high for me to act on it. I didn't even know if Anderson was still here. Maybe he'd had enough. Maybe he'd gone home. Maybe that's what he wanted me to think.

I wanted to pull my hair out. I couldn't even get up to make a fresh pot of coffee without the risk of missing something important. I had to fight to keep my heavy eyelids from drooping over my eyes with sheer willpower. The fear was still there, sure, but I wasn't sleeping

BODYCAM

before, and now with nothing to really spike my adrenaline since Anderson disappeared, my body was trying to get some much-needed rest.

No. I couldn't. I shook my head. I paced around the room, glancing furtively at the TV screen, which was showing a view of the backyard patio. I sat down again and watched Heather's little shoulders move in sync with her soft breathing. I turned back to the TV and alternated through the channels again. I came up to my bedroom window and saw something, but my thumb hit the button again to the view from across the street. Startled, I switched back, and I stared at the back of Anderson's head silhouetted by the light behind a layer of curtains and venetian blinds. I felt my heart sink in a way I'd never felt before, like it was retreating from the reality of the situation. I turned my head toward the window just a few feet from the TV. Somehow, even though I couldn't see him, I could *feel* him there. Standing perfectly still. Peering through the curtains, the venetian blinds, past the TV, *at me.*

ALEXANDER ENGEL-HODGKINSON

I hadn't realized I'd been holding my breath. I shuddered as I exhaled slowly, my eyes snapping back to Anderson's shadow over my window. Just standing there... about twelve inches from the left—my left. Slowly, without getting up from the bed, my fingers curled around the grip of my revolver. Double-action—no need to waste precious effort working my thumb on the hammer after all those hours pushing buttons on the remote control. Just point... God, calculate it just *right*... aim... shoot.

I heard Elaine call my name from a hollow distance and nearly fired my weapon. It came from the TV. The TV said my name in her voice. I looked at it. The picture was the same. The timecode was running uninterrupted. Anderson was still there. Staring through the window. Twelve inches from the left. My left. I raised the gun. Elaine said my name again, her voice crackling through the TV's speakers. She sounded like she was in pain, crying for help from some metallic chamber. Concentrate. Aim. Twelve inches from my left. At the window.

A loud crash, but not from the

BODYCAM

revolver—from the other end of the house. Feet pounded through the living room. Glass shattered as the ruckus entered the hall. I looked at the TV just as Anderson's head ducked back into the black outline around the window.

Twenty-second delay.

Rapid footfalls raced straight for us and I whirled with the gun as Anderson threw open the door and his shotgun howled at me. Heather shrieked as I felt my flesh tear out of my right shoulder and I dropped the gun. No! No! Anderson bared his teeth at Heather like some wild animal. He called her a whore and rambled unintelligibly—something about his family, the whores tearing his family apart? Temptation? Temptress! *Whore!*—as he chambered another round into his shotgun and pointed it at her. I could've gone for the gun. I *should've* gone for the gun. I threw myself over Heather instead, my revolver abandoned, my instinct kicking in, making me stupid, making me afraid. Now we were both going to die and I held my screaming daughter against me and buried her face in my chest.

ALEXANDER ENGEL-HODGKINSON

"Don't look," I was telling her. "Don't look. It'll be over soon."

It wasn't. The shot never came. Not for *us*. I looked up at Anderson, but Anderson wasn't looking at me. He was looking at the TV, and I turned my head and looked at what he saw, and what we saw was Elaine's indecipherable mask of hate, love, fear, pain, and joy spilling through the television screen like internal organs out of a deer that'd been slit open. Her bulging eyes with tiny pupils were fixed on Anderson. The body that followed her head into our world wasn't gelatinous like it was before; now it was a solid abomination, a hundred Elaines mashed and crumpled together to form a long, centipede-like body with hundreds of her arms and legs extending from her flanks. She undulated grotesquely around the foot of the bed and then rose up, straightening her frontward segments that towered above all three of us. Her multiple torsos were maps of faces, Elaine's faces, all wearing that same unreadable expression—all *staring* at us. More of her was still coming out of the TV, spooling around the foot of the bed until there wasn't enough room on the floor, and then piling on the end of the bed.

Then she just... stopped. Heather turned her head and didn't say anything. She didn't even breathe. Neither did I, as my arms tightened around her. We were pressed against the headboard, watching this *thing*, waiting for it to move, to do *something*.

Anderson's jaw was working, but no sound came out of his mouth. He was rooted to the spot, holding the shotgun like he had no intention of using it. Or he'd forgotten it was even there after seeing... this...

God. Those eyes. They didn't blink. Some were fixed on me. Some watched Heather. Others, including the larger head at the centipede's forefront, were watching Anderson. Occasionally the twisted, compacted torsos that made up the thing's body rippled in random spasmodic fits, as if each one were feeling its own individual pain.

Anderson screamed with a kind of primal fear I'd never heard from another human being before. He raised the shotgun but the Elaine-thing *lunged* at him, slithering so fast he didn't squeeze off a shot, just turned and bolted out of the room, still screaming that primal scream with a thousand Elaines in pursuit. Their faces blurred past Heather and I like individual frames in a moving picture film, contorting with rage. That indecipherable mask shattered a horrible memory replaced by something so much worse, worse than I know how to describe. The last of her scuttled down the hall and I heard Anderson screaming in the backyard. I lunged for the remote control, sweat-slicked fingers unable to grip it, like it was a wet bar of soap. And they were shaking so much, I struggled to flick through the surveillance channels, but I did manage, just as Anderson's screams filled the night around us. I reached one of the backyard cams. He didn't make it past the fire pit. She caught up with him and *broke into segments*, surrounded him, grabbed each of his limbs as the segments spiraled off the ground in perfect sync and they started tearing him to pieces and—

BODYCAM

Heather was watching. I told her to look away. She didn't seem to know I was there. I grabbed her and held her close and hid her eyes from the TV. I noticed then that Anderson's screams had only been silenced outside. On the TV, he was gurgling loudly, sickeningly. The grainy quality of the night vision feed was showing a writhing, massive blob in the middle of the backyard, and when Anderson stopped screaming through the TV the mass of writhing crooked limbs had calmed, somewhat.

Now she—*it* was unspooling across the backyard the same way ripples spread in water after a stone breached its surface. She skidded toward the camera, her face enlarging on the screen, her eye pressing against the lens. The screen surged, as if it were offering some kind of resistance against her, before giving way to her face, which stretched through the screen, the edges of the TV pulling her skin back as she pushed through.

She was coming back for us!

Heather whimpered, petrified, as more of that thing, now bigger than before, squeezed through with an obscene moan rumbling from its throat at a deep, distorted pitch. I threw Heather on the bed and dived for the shotgun and snatched it up. I whirled, aimed, and blasted the TV to pieces, firing, chambering, firing, chambering, firing until there weren't any shells left to fire. Elaine screeched as the TV, the VCR, and the cable box exploded to pieces behind her and the fleshy portion of her that managed to come through splattered onto the floor like a slab of raw, wet meat, severed from the body.

But what about the rest of her? I clambered across the bed and picked up the .38, ignoring the searing pain in my shoulder, and I ran to the bedroom doorway but nothing was coming down the hall. I ran to the window behind where the TV was in the corner, next to the one Anderson was looking through, and I drew aside the curtain and the venetian blinds to see dozens of twisted black things scattering into the dark woods like phantoms, merging with the shadows without leaving a trace of themselves or Anderson behind.

Half of Elaine's face twitched on the

BODYCAM

blood-soaked carpet, surrounded by bone shards and fragments of cartilage. The one eye that came through stared lifelessly at the ceiling.

I *hoped* it was lifeless…

ALEXANDER ENGEL-HODGKINSON

MONDAY/OCTOBER 6TH/1997
AM 00:03:33:33

I was already awake, shivering from cold sweats. I couldn't remember the last time I slept well. Not since... since August. A few hours here, a few minutes there. Occasionally my body would shut down for about ten or so hours. It happened frequently enough over the following months that Heather learned to pack her own lunch, brush her teeth, get dressed, and step on the bus without my supervision. The first few times she let me sleep, I woke up to an empty house and panicked. I called the school first and they confirmed she was in class. The principal was vaguely aware of the circumstances since February, since Elaine's attack, and Anderson's intrusion; and was very understanding. With my hesitant permission, the principal, Mrs. Hartford, introduced Heather to the school's child psychologist, Dr. Martha Campbell.

Heather had become withdrawn since the incident, eating very little and sleeping even less than I was, and when she did fall asleep she woke up screaming. She didn't

BODYCAM

hang out with her friends. In fact, she talked to almost no one. Even Dr. Campbell struggled to maintain a conversation with her during their first few weeks. Patience, she told me, and just the right amount of attention. She needed to know that she was safe in her own home, after all. My fears were realized when Heather eventually opened up about the monster that looked like her mother, and Anderson's death, and numerous strange happenings leading up to it. Luckily she wasn't aware that someone had been watching her through her window—I assumed it was Anderson all this time. Heather didn't understand the complexities of the whole thing. But the part that I was really worried about, was the time she saw me standing in front of my TV after that thing attacked me. I knew what it would look like to anyone who heard that story. I expected child services to take her away at any given moment. They never came. Heather either forgot about it or never mentioned it. Either way I was grateful that she was never taken from me.

Anderson hadn't tampered with the

car. I discovered that the same morning after that whole incident, after I burned half of Elaine's face in the fire pit and filled in the hole where I'd been discarding the tapes. I took Heather with me to the police station and reported a saner version of events—that Anderson had been stalking me and had installed cameras around my property, changing the story so that Anderson shot the TV, the VCR, and the cable box. I told them that when he ran out of shells and saw that he'd missed us both (I mentioned that he was raving like he'd gone insane), and saw the gun in my possession, he fled into the woods. I provided them with the necessary permit for my .38, of course. They went on to tell me how lucky I was, how fortunate Heather was, despite the obvious trauma something like that would inflict on a young child. If only they knew. If only I could've told them the truth. I knew no one would believe us.

We spent several weeks in a hotel until we were comfortable enough to go back home. I pulled extra shifts at the gas station to keep out of financial debt. Hotels

BODYCAM

are expensive as hell to stay in for that long.

Pastor Clemens visited on numerous occasions. Wellness check, he'd always say. We would have coffee and talk about things, anything except the whole affair with the Andersons, and why they hated us so much. Why they were so goddamned weird.

I wondered why they did what they did all the time. I wracked my brain for a reason behind that insanity. The police didn't say much in their follow-up after they investigated the scene at the house. There were indeed cameras all over the place, but they apparently weren't connected to anything. They couldn't be traced to a source. And with my own surveillance equipment destroyed in the incident, there was no physical evidence to be found, aside from the shattered patio screen door, the damaged bedroom door, and my shoulder wound; the latter obviously wasn't self-inflicted.

The police searched for Anderson, but like his wife, they couldn't find any trace of them. They even unearthed the videotapes I'd buried behind the backyard, having briefly suspected me of murdering them both, as I was the last person to see them alive. I was questioned, but the evidence just wasn't there. Any acts of aggression against the Andersons were clearly self-defence. And when their past involvement with a transhumanist cult came to light, they figured mental illness was the most obvious explanation. The Andersons were crazy, and clearly, despite everything that'd happened I was still very much in control of myself.

I'd heard later that the Anderson sons were left in the care of distant relatives in Toronto. Their house was abandoned. The family didn't seem to want the property, and no one seemed interested in buying or selling it. Nobody said anything, but everyone knew the string of violent rapes ended with the disappearance of the Andersons; there was little doubt they had something to do with the attacks. The parents were most likely dead, or in hiding. Without confirmation, without bodies, there was a frightened hush among the locals. Nobody talked about it. Nobody wanted to give it much thought. I knew for sure that

BODYCAM

Mr. Anderson had been killed by whatever that thing was, that thing that resembled Elaine, but I had no idea what had happened to Donna.

I never got another TV. That meant no surveillance camera, no VCR. I stopped getting videotapes, anyway, so there was no longer any need for that stuff. The weird happenings weren't happening anymore. Gradually, the emptiness of the house wasn't so overwhelming anymore, as time dulled the pain of Elaine's passing. I kept replaying that moment in my head, when that thing attacked Anderson, and I thought back even further to that time when I saw a similar creature watching Heather sleep until I discovered it. It could've torn us both to shreds anytime it wanted to, but it didn't. It retreated back inside the TV. I wondered if that was Elaine, somehow transferred into...

No. That's impossible. A guy could go crazy trying to make sense of something like that.

I called Clemens, and when he finally answered he asked me if I knew what time it was. I felt bad, then. I'd totally lost track of the time. It was almost four in the morning. I apologized and was about to hang up when he asked me why I was calling him, as he may as well know now that he was up. I invited him and his family over for dinner. He said in a good-natured tone that he'd speak to Andrea about it and call me back at a decent hour with an answer.

So I sat there in the dark, trying to think about nice things. I went into the kitchen and made myself some coffee. I checked on Heather and caught the Anderson boy hanging halfway through the window, eyes wide as saucers, reflecting the hallway light as I'd opened the door, his gloved hand extended toward my daughter.

Instantly I rushed at him and he pulled himself back out into the backyard, dragging the venetian blinds out with him. Heather started awake, totally confused and scared. I leaned out the window as the Anderson boy took off running across the backyard. Heather started crying and asked me what was happening. I told her everything was fine. I told her to lock the window behind me. Then I inelegantly

BODYCAM

climbed over the window sill and felt the soft earth give slightly under my slippers. I charged after the Anderson boy as he darted into the shadows. I considered only for a second that those other things had scattered in these same woods. The next second, I remembered that I didn't have my gun. I didn't care. I caught the little creep in the act, trying to snatch my daughter, to do God knows what to her. He was a moving shape in the darkness as he tried to lose me in the trees. We stumbled in the dark, tripping over roots and rocks and things. The Anderson boy wheezed loudly as he led me into a clearing, and when I entered the clearing I looked up and saw the backside of a two-storey house. He was running full-tilt for the back door and practically threw himself into it, skidded on his feet when he turned around to slam the door shut, but I was on him by then. I drove my shoulder into it and sent him sprawling across the white tiles of a kitchen floor. He was whining the whole time as he crawled down a hallway and I followed him to a door under the stairs, bellowing furiously at him, asking him why.

ALEXANDER ENGEL-HODGKINSON

"Why were you in my daughter's room? What were you trying to do to her? What were you *doing* in there?!"

"Stop, please!" he sniveled. "Don't come any closer!" He grabbed a nearby picture frame and flung it at me. I ducked to avoid it. That bought him enough time to open the door under the stairs. It looked unusually strong, and I caught a glimpse of the inner layer which had a dull sheen of painted metal. Some kind of panic room? It didn't matter because I managed to get a good kick in before he could close it between us. He tumbled down a flight of wooden stairs. I looked down. I could hear my pulse thundering in my ears. He wasn't moving. I didn't know his name, so I called down to him as "Kid?"

Still no answer. He didn't even twitch. "Kid?"

Slowly, I descended into the basement, each step creaking and bending under my weight. I got within three steps of him curled up on the landing and stopped. He still hadn't moved. I wondered if I killed him. I went down two more steps and kicked his shin, and got no

BODYCAM

response.

There was no light down here except for the hallway light above. I went back up the stairs and found a light switch and flicked it on. That's when I saw how the Anderson boy's head was sandwiched between his shoulders and the wall, angled weirdly. His eyes were wide open, mouth agape. I knew then that he was dead.

Slowly, I went back down the stairs, stupidly considering checking for a pulse, even though it was obvious. I turned to go back up and saw the strangest thing... a lab of sorts, with one section separated from rows of steel shelves stocked full with videotapes. The separate section was surrounded by black curtains. I could see a tiny sliver of red light between the curtains.

I should've gone back up, but I didn't. The boy was dead. No one else was here. The boy wasn't even supposed to be here. So I climbed down to the cold concrete floor and perused one of the aisles of videotapes in clamshell cases, hands at my sides, glancing at the labels on the cases' spines:

MY HOUSE;

ALEXANDER ENGEL-HODGKINSON

CARMICHAEL HOUSE;
CLEMENS HOUSE;
MORGAN HOUSE;
CAVANAUGH HOUSE;
…and there were several more, including my own. When I saw one of several tapes with my house on them, I pulled it out of its spot and studied the photograph on the case, at the bottom of which was a sticker with ELAINE SEX handwritten in black permanent marker. I took another one off the shelf: ELAINE SHOWER. More of them: HEATHER SHOWER; HEATHER CHANGING; ELAINE FUCKING; ELAINE FUCKING; HEATHER CHANGING; ELAINE AND ME FUCKING; ELAINE AND ME FUCKING; DIE ELAINE DIE FUCKING DAD AND ME.

I dropped the tapes on the floor, stunned. I went over the CLEMENS HOUSE section: ANDREA NUDE; ANDREA FUCKING; ANDREA CHANGING; MARIA (Andrea's daughter) CHANGING. Jesus. Jesus. I went to the CAVANAUGH HOUSE section: SARAH (the daughter) CHANGING; SARAH

BODYCAM

FUCKING; DAD AND SARAH FUCKING; and too many with gold stars stickered all over them, all reading like: SARAH AND ME FUCKING; SARAH AND ME FUCKING; SARAH AND ME FUCKING; DIE SARAH FUCKING ME SUCK MY FUCKING COCK WHORE FUCKING BITCH FUCK YOU.

My legs gave out under me. I collapsed on my hands and knees and started to sob. I was surrounded by these things… all of these… *things*. I retched, tasting bile. No… no, don't throw up.

Despite my repulsion and overwhelming disgust, I checked some of the labels on the tapes in the MY HOUSE section. All of their names were written on various tapes—some were of the parents, some involved their daughter and the father, some the daughter and the brother, and then I regretted looking and turned away.

The red room behind the curtain had a water basin and photographs clipped to a clothesline under a red lamp. On the other side of the basement was the Anderson girl chained to a mattress in the corner. She wasn't in one piece, and she seemed to have been dead for a while. Again, I fought the urge to vomit. I wiped my fingerprints off of everything I touched, carefully replaced the videotapes on the shelves, and avoided touching the Anderson boy's corpse on my way up. I wanted to spit on him. I wanted to drive my heel through his sick fucking skull just to make sure he was dead, but I knew it already. His neck was broken. I didn't mean to kill him, but after… after *that*… I didn't regret it.

I left the Anderson house and crossed through the woods. I thought I saw Elaine standing in the dark among the thinner trees, stretched so that she was a lot taller than I remembered her. I did a double-take. It was just an odd-looking tree.

Somehow I managed to keep it together until I returned home. I stopped at the fire pit and threw up in it. Once that was out of my system, I called Heather's name from the patio but I didn't get any answer. I went to her bedroom window, but it was shut and locked and the curtain was pulled over it again. I called out to her. Still no response.

Now I was worried. I knocked on the

BODYCAM

window again and called her name even louder. The curtains were suddenly swept aside, and I saw her face looking frightfully at me behind the glass. Then she ran out of the room and a few seconds later the patio light came on. She leaned her head out and I rushed over and hugged her so tightly that she complained I was suffocating her. I apologized and kissed her all over. I couldn't stop myself from crying, and she cried, too. For the first time in a very long time, they weren't tears of grief.

It *was* over now, I think. The Andersons were all dead. I hated leaving the Anderson girl's body there, but if I made a report after my recent history with them, they'd suspect foul play. They might not rule the Anderson boy's death as an accident. And I just couldn't allow that. Not after everything that'd happened. No one comes between me and my daughter.

I cleaned myself up, stuffing everything I wore to the Anderson house into a garbage bag, and put on a fresh pot of coffee to calm my nerves. At seven, I woke up Heather and took her with me on a drive to Orillia. I tossed the garbage bag into a dumpster outside of a Holiday Inn. Then we returned home.

Clemens called back around nine-thirty in the morning. He said they'd love to join us for dinner.

They brought homemade potato salad and homemade pumpkin pie. The four of us sat around the table and ate some meat lasagna I prepared. Store-bought, of course. I was never any kind of original chef. Lawrence and Andrea looked happy together. Like one couldn't live without the other. It reminded me of how things were between Elaine and I. It was a bittersweet thing, the two of them. I was happy for them. Really.

After dinner, they helped us clean up despite my insisting they leave it all to me. We socialized, and Heather was thrilled with the prospect of staying up past her bedtime.

After they left, I put Heather to bed. "Marley will keep the bad dreams away," I told her, as I tucked the bear under her chin. "And Daddy will keep the real-life monsters away."

"Promise?"

BODYCAM

"I promise, sweetheart. Go to sleep, now." I kissed her forehead and left her door open by a crack. I left my own bedroom door open as I dressed for bed. I happened to notice the picture frame on the dresser had been set upright. Elaine's wedding photo. She was smiling beautifully on the happiest day of our lives. Well, second-happiest, behind the day Heather came into this world. I reached over to set it face-down on the dresser.

No. I changed my mind...

ALEXANDER ENGEL-HODGKINSON

AFTERWORD

Sometimes I would fall asleep watching movies and wake up totally bewildered in a dark room with the TV screen blinding me and disorienting me further. I always hated waking up to that. When I was a kid, things like *The Ring* or that scene in one of those *A Wrinkle in Time* adaptations where Mrs. Whatsit contacted Charles Wallace through a fucking television set terrified me. Something about otherworldly interferences with technology used to keep me up at night. Ghostly smears in photographs, surveillance footage with weird shapes in them; whatever it was, I was probably scared of it at one time or another. Kayako from *Ju-on* used to be one of my biggest childhood fears, just from the pictures and a trailer for the remake—that horrible death rattle!

Then I watched the movie and it sucked. The original is slightly better. But the way she distorts the TV news broadcast

BODYCAM

in the Japanese original still sends chills down my spine. And Sadako is another matter entirely... *The Ring* and its Japanese original *Ringu* were among my first forays into horror involving videotapes and other late nineties/early 2000's technology, and their aesthetic never really left my mind over a decade later. I didn't want to plummet into any of the same pitfalls I could remember from those movies while writing *Bodycam* where the protagonists actively searched for a cause and clear understanding behind the curse. I never found that to be scary. In fact, I thought it made everything *less* scary.

I feel like a lot of horror betrays itself by showing far too much, and sometimes I think other works betray themselves and the audience by showing too little. It's very hard to strike a good balance between the two. I don't know if I've struck it with *She Watches Me Bury Her* and *Bodycam* because what one person might find terrifying might bore somebody else. I just go with what scares me and jump off from there.

Around this time, I've been working

on four things at once all the time. Feels
like I'm getting nothing done sometimes,
considering how long it takes to finish one
thing. I dedicated two unbroken weeks to
write *Bodycam* from beginning to end in the
middle of writing *Death Under
Candyland's Eye*, itself a break from *Cobalt
Rogue, Vol. 3.5: Hell Week*; the latter two
I've completed well over 400 pages in each.
Hell, I've been working on those two
halves of *CR, Vol. 3* for six years now. It
feels like it's never going to end. Yet for
some reason as I approach the end of
everything I start, I want to start something
else. Quite problematic.

I have a lot of ideas and concepts I'd
like to explore in between *Cobalt Rogue*
volumes. I have an entire folder full of
smaller side projects like this one just
waiting for a couple weeks' dedication to
their completion. A lot of side projects
around the larger *Cobalt Rogue* novels, and
I guess the occasional full-length novel like
Candyland's Eye (which has turned out to
be a lot longer than I originally intended). I
even have an entire timeline mapped out for
Cobalt Rogue long after the *Final*

BODYCAM

Apocalypse Saga's end.

Most of my stories take place in two separate universes, though one is sometimes vaguely affected by the other in ways I don't want to get into just yet—or ever. It all depends on what I finish in the end. I doubt if I'll get a third of it all done, but I'd kinda like for them all to see the light of day sometime.

I hope you all enjoy what's to come.

-2021

ALEXANDER ENGEL-HODGKINSON

Works by Alexander Engel-Hodgkinson

Clockworld (One-Shot)
I Keep My True Love in the Basement (One-Shot)
Reality Glitch ('Jumping for Charlotte' segment)
No Bounds ('Cranston & Layman' segment)

The Final Apocalypse Saga
(IN CHRONOLOGICAL ORDER)
Cobalt Rogue, Vol. 1: The Dead Blue
Cobalt Rogue, Vol. 2: Sky Japan Welcome Party
Cobalt Rogue, Vol. 3: Cemetery Rumble, Part I
Cobalt Rogue, Vol. 3.5: Hell Week (Coming Soon)
Post-Apocalyptic Days
Cobalt Christmas
I Keep My True Love in the Basement/REMIX

ZYKLON IV Continuum
(IN CHRONOLOGICAL ORDER)
Bodycam
She Watches Me Bury Her
The Laughter in the Woods (Coming Soon)
The Tea Party Affair
Jumping for Charlotte
Death Under Candyland's Eye